When Reindeer Sing

Merry Christmas
and
HAPPY NEW YEAR
(no matter how you sing it)

It was almost the day of the big production at the North Pole. Everyone was planning to record a new song to show the world the true meaning of Christmas.

So, of course, it needed to be perfect.

During practice,

the elves were excellent.

The snowmen were superb.

Even Mrs. Claus was marvelous.

And everyone was happy, until they realized something was off.

What is that awful noise?

And it was very, very off.

It was the reindeer.
They were terrible.

And, they were the loudest of them all.

An emergency meeting was called to decide what to do.

The elves were angry.

The snowmen were sad.

Even Mrs. Claus was concerned because...

they didn't know what to do.

The song was far from perfect. And, no one was happy anymore.

It was decided. While Santa kept the reindeer distracted, everyone else would record the song in secret without the reindeer.

It was the only way to make the song perfect again.

While the others recorded the song, Santa and the reindeer made snow angels together. The reindeer were so happy that they sang with glee, and more than a little off key.

"Ho, Ho, Ho, that's awful," Santa whispered to himself.

When they decorated the tree, the reindeer sang merrily, and still quite painfully.

During hide-and-seek, the reindeer couldn't hide because they sang with lots of pride.

"We're just so happy," the reindeer replied.
"We love to sing about Christmas time."

Hmmm. They do seem happy.

Later that night, Santa could hardly eat his dinner.

"What's wrong, dear," Mrs. Claus asked.

"I have prevented the reindeer from doing something they loved because I decided it wasn't good enough," he said. "I'm the one who missed the true meaning of Christmas."

Maybe it's not too late to change things.

Santa called another meeting to tell the others they needed to include the reindeer. "Everyone at the North Pole should get to be a part of the song," he said.

But I thought we wanted to bring joy to the world, not sadness.

The very next day, the North Pole made a new recording. It was the loudest and proudest, the most joyful and beautiful, because it had included everyone.

And when the world heard it, they all sang along.

Nobody worried about singing it wrong.

Oh joy! Finally a song that's impossible to sing out of tune, even when you try really, really hard!

And everyone agreed. The song was Christmas, especially the parts that were definitely, and most merrily, more than a little off key.

Nice work, Reindeer!

Overjoyed to help, Santa.

Merry Christmas!

Made in the USA
Middletown, DE
18 September 2020